MENACE
AND
MISCHIEF

SYLVIA GUNNERY

Stoddart Kids
TORONTO • NEW YORK

For Hobo's friends at Hebbville Junior High School
in Lunenburg County, Nova Scotia,
from 1991 to 1994.

We gratefully acknowledge the Canada Council for the Arts
and the Ontario Arts Council for their support
of our publishing program.

Published in Canada in 1999 by
Stoddart Kids,
a division of Stoddart Publishing Co. Limited
34 Lesmill Road
Toronto, Canada M3B 2T6
Tel. (416) 445-3333 Fax (416) 445-5967
E-mail Customer.Service@ccmailgw.genpub.com

Published in the United States in 1999 by
Stoddart Kids,
a division of Stoddart Publishing Co. Limited
180 Varick Street, 9th Floor
New York, New York 10014
Toll free 1-800-805-1083
E-mail gdsinc@genpub.com

Distributed in Canada by
General Distribution Services
325 Humber College Blvd.
Toronto, Canada M9W 7C3
Tel. (416) 213-1919 Fax (416) 213-1917
E-mail Customer.Service@ccmailgw.genpub.com

Distributed in the United States by
General Distribution Services
85 River Rock Drive, Suite 202
Buffalo, New York 14207
Toll free 1-800-805-1083
E-mail gdsinc@genpub.com

Canadian Cataloguing in Publication Data
Gunnery, Sylvia
Menance and mischief

ISBN 0-7736-7477-2
I. Title.
PS8563.U575M46 1999   jC813'.54   C98-932526-1
PZ7.G84Me 1999

Cover illustration: Judith Christine Mills
Cover and text design: Tannice Goddard
Computer layout: Mary Bowness

Printed and bound in Canada

Chapter 1

Schemes and Dreams

C. J. was writing in his journal. In the classroom, he could hear the sound of pens scraping across pages. Everyone was writing — Mr. Saunders' way of starting every single English class.

Someone was sniffing . . . and sniffing.

Then Raymond moved his legs and knocked his knees against his desk again. There wasn't a desk in the whole school big enough to accommodate Raymond's giraffe legs.

In this very quiet room, a person could almost detect Hobo's snoring — if hamsters actually do snore while sleeping under mounds of wood shavings all day.

And did C. J. just hear Julie sigh? A sweet, soft, melodic sigh?

He couldn't think in so much silence. His brain was full of junk, probably the most boring junk anyone in the entire grade seven class had ever written.

"Time! Put your journals away and let's play ball."

Some teachers are born to educate. Not Mr. Saunders. He wasn't born to be a baseball player, either, even though he made everything sound like an inning of the World Series. He was actually born to be a writer — a poet, in fact. But no one else knew about that secret dream. Yet.

"Today we'll entertain ourselves with the most profound poem the Muses have inspired in this century — 'Casey At The Bat'!"

Clarence James opened his textbook and tried to keep his mind off the thunder of hunger rumbling in his stomach. Recess was only thirty-five poetic minutes away.

* * *

Raymond came rushing out of the library where he'd just borrowed an oversized volume about rare tropical fish. He knew he'd be late for science class if he didn't break the speed limit.

Just around the corner, out of Raymond's

sight, Wilson, Terry, and Jay were ambling in slow-motion to their next class. Being almost late was one of the reputations those three grade nines had worked hard to maintain.

When Raymond saw them, he instantly realized he wasn't going to be able to stop before collision. The three grade nines only had time to open their drowsy eyes in shock before their world collided with Raymond's. There was a sudden chaos of ooofs and gasps and falling books. Above the din, a bell blasted to begin period three.

In an instant, the vice-principal was on the scene, assessing the damage and concluding that there was none. "Young man," she said to Raymond, "you've just learned the hard way that there's a reason we ask students not to run in the halls of Haliburton Junior High School."

"He just about killed us!" protested Wilson.

Terry and Jay were lifting themselves up from the floor and rubbing sore elbows.

"Now let's just study this situation," Ms. Cameron said. "You three gentlemen aren't where you should be. Seems to me it's a case of being in the wrong place at the wrong time. And I do mean wrong time. Must be your second late this week, Wilson. And it's only Tuesday. Same for your cohorts, no doubt. I'm grounding all of you at noonhour. Maybe this young man in grade seven is just learning about the Haliburton rules, but you grade nines have been around a long while. Too long, if my blood pressure is any indication of it. There's no excuse for you to be late."

Raymond smiled. It wasn't that he was smirking at those grade nine guys. No. It had to do with the way the vice-principal had given her long speech. And then the bit about her blood pressure. That was a good one.

The trouble with smiling is that sometimes people don't know what you're really smiling about.

Wilson's eyes narrowed, and he did something with his teeth that made him look like he was chewing on a leather slipper. It reminded Raymond of his aunt's bulldog.

When he arrived at science class, Raymond still felt uneasy. He tried flipping through the colorful photographs of rare and elegant tropical fish. But in his mind were those narrow eyes and those teeth grinding in anger.

At noonhour, he saw the three grade nines in the detention room next to the office. What a relief! He didn't yet realize that he was now their enemy. A challenge to their authority. An obstacle they couldn't ignore.

* * *

"Julie! Wait —" Suddenly C.J. stopped. Someone else had walked up behind Julie and now was putting a hand on her arm. She turned around.

Wilson! Tall, dark, always-cool-looking Wilson. He was standing right beside Julie with a big grin on his face. She was looking up at him like she was Alice in Wonderland and he was the Cheshire Cat. Like she was lost and he knew the way out of the forest.

C. J.'s heart gave a squeeze, a flutter, and then seemed to lie down on its back and slip into a coma.

They didn't talk for long, but even after Wilson had walked away, C. J. had lost his urge to catch up to Julie. He'd been planning to ask her to go with him to the dance on Thursday. For almost two days he'd been rehearsing the words — in the shower, or waiting for the bus, or watching the back of her head in science class.

He had planned to say something like this: Hey, Julie. (That part he would say slow, casual-like.) You going to the dance on Thursday? (This would sound as if he himself might not go, but then again maybe he might.) Wanna go with me? We both have to get drives and my father said he'd take us. (This part would sound like it was just a convenient arrangement, not like a serious date — because how serious could it be with his dad as a chauffeur?)

Then it hit him like a plummeting asteroid — Wilson had probably just asked Julie to go to the dance with him!

He could practically hear the whole conversation in his head: Hey, Julie babe. You wanna be seen with the coolest guy in school when you walk into the dance on Thursday night?

Huh?

Well, maybe Julie wouldn't say something as stunned as Huh?, but for sure she would be shocked if Wilson actually did ask her for a date.

C. J. couldn't stand the suspense. She was still by herself, so he strolled over.

"Hey, Julie. I just saw you talking to that Wilson guy. Did he ask you to go to the dance?"

"No."

"Well, it looked like —"

"You're jumping to conclusions, C.J. He just asked me if I was going to the dance. That's all."

"That's all! It practically means you two have a date. Get with it, Julie. Why else would a guy stop a girl and start talking about the dance?"

"I don't know, C. J. Why?"

"'Cause he wants a date? Why else?"

"So's that why you're talking to me about the dance right now?"

C. J. sent a fast fax to his brain, begging it not to make him blush. Next time he'd better try e-mail — his brain didn't get the message on time.

Blushing was the third most irritating thing on his list of things he'd change about himself if he could. Second on that list was how short he still was, even though he was thirteen. What bugged him most of all was actually two things, but he thought of them as a matched pair: his blond hair and blue eyes. Put together, they made him look like a kind of cross between one of Santa's elves and a Cabbage Patch Kid.

"I just wanted to warn you, that's all," he said and walked away, trying to look like a guy who's known a girl for seven years and wants to be like a big brother to her. Not like a guy who's had a crush on a girl for seven years and can't quite get the nerve to let her know.

At the main entrance of the school, he almost slammed into Raymond who had his nose stuck in that book about tropical fish. C. J. pretended to be out of breath so Raymond wouldn't make a big deal out of the blush that still soaked his cheeks.

"What's the rush?"

"Didn't want to miss my bus," said C. J., huffing and puffing.

Raymond took his nose out of the book and looked at his watch. "You got ten minutes before your bus gets here."

"Oh really? Oh. Well. No rush, then, I guess."

"You see Julie?" asked Raymond.

"Julie? Ah, well, yea, I think I saw her somewhere in the halls. I was running so fast I can't be sure."

"Maybe I missed her."

"Missed her? What does that mean?"

Raymond closed the tropical fish book and glanced furtively over his shoulder. C. J. thought it meant he was going to tell a secret, but actually he was on the lookout for Wilson, Terry, and Jay. Although his noonhour had been a safe one, he hadn't escaped them altogether. When he'd left gym class to get a drink of water, there they'd been, sauntering out of the washroom.

"Hey, Knees!" Wilson had yelled.

The two others picked up the joke — "Knees. Knees. Knees." Their taunt had sounded like the shrill cawing of crows. "We're going to get you, Knees. No one makes us waste a whole noonhour in detention and gets away with it."

Without taking a drink, Raymond had hurried back into the gymnasium. There, he looked down in the direction of his knees, noticing for the first time that they were like misplaced lumps on his long, skinny legs. They reminded him of seagull knees.

"What do you mean you missed Julie?" C. J. asked again. "Are you waiting for her?"

"Yea."

"Why?"

"Thought I'd ask her to go to the dance with me."

C. J. couldn't believe what he was hearing. This was crazy! Raymond was practically like Julie's brother! They'd been in the same class since kindergarten! He couldn't have a crush —

But he could. Of course he could. Just like C. J. did. Just like Wilson did.

"I think Wilson asked her. You know Wilson? He's that grade nine guy who always hangs out with two other goons. They act like they own the whole school."

Raymond's mouth gaped open, giving him the appearance of a hungry tropical fish. Dirty looks, threats, and stupid nicknames were bad enough. Now, Wilson was howling through Raymond's heart and trying to steal Julie!

"You sure?"

"Practically. He asked her if she was going to the dance and that's just like saying he'll see her there and it'll be a date."

When the bus arrived, Julie sat at the back with two of her friends. C. J. stayed at the front and talked to the driver about how much gas an average bus burned in an average week. He managed to make himself look interested in this boring conversation. At least it gave him an excuse to avoid further discussion with Julie about dates and dances.

Raymond, who didn't take the bus, was

already halfway across the school lawn, heading home, as the bus pulled away. His usual route took him past a small park where the river curled close to the road. It was quiet there, with shallow water slipping over rocks and sliding underneath low tree branches. He was almost always alone there.

On a large pine tree, someone had hung a swing made from an old tire on the end of a thick, long rope. Raymond balanced one foot in the tire and grabbed the rope with both hands. The small movements back and forth soon gained momentum and he was soaring out over the river, and then back. Out and up. Down and back. Water and sky. Pine needles and pebbles.

His thoughts were so far away that he nearly lost his grip on the rope when he saw a person standing, almost hiding, beside one of the picnic tables.

He scraped his foot on the ground to stop the swing.

The person turned quickly and hurried out of the park, but Raymond knew exactly who it was: Terry. Maybe he'd taken off to get Wilson and Jay.

Without looking back, Raymond rushed home.

* * *

C. J. settled down to stare at the T.V. but he had his own soap opera scene playing in his mind: Wilson held Julie in his grade nine Mafia arms.

Self-pity crept into his heart and taped posters to the wall of his left ventricle: Julie loves Wilson. Wilson loves Julie. C. J. loses his first love.

Suddenly, a rush of fresh energy swept through him. What if he just stepped out of the picture so Raymond could have Julie? Then at least Wilson wouldn't have her. Besides, if best friends liked the same person, maybe it wouldn't be long before they weren't best friends anymore. That was it, then. His decision was made. He'd save Julie from the suave moves of Wilson by showing her that it was Raymond she really loved!

A lightbulb went on in C. J.'s brain and just about blew a fuse: what if Julie received a love letter from Raymond? It would be a simple letter, well-worded, not too gushy, and it would convince her that Raymond was the guy for her.

Yes! He went to his bedroom and took out pen and paper.

* * *

It was dark in the empty classrooms and hall-ways of Haliburton Junior High. Too dark to see the clock on the wall of Mr. Saunders' classroom. It was 2:38 a.m. Hobo stepped into her exercise wheel and ran. She ran uphill, up, up, and up, getting nowhere. She might've been thinking about how frustrating this was, or she might've been imagining racing up the knolls and slopes of a forest. Or she might not have been thinking at all.

Down through the blackness of the hall and around the corner was the science lab. There, in a glass cage, was Ms. Harrison's pet boa constrictor, Miss Hiss, thick and still, curled warmly against herself. A dream rippled the scales of her beautifully patterned skin.

As boa constrictors often do, Miss Hiss had been sleeping for almost a week. Not because she was lazy. Not because she was bored. She had been digesting her favorite delicacy: mmmouth-watering, mmmedium-sized mmmice.

Her dark eye peered into the pitch-black night. Maybe she was thinking about how small her glass cage was, or maybe she was imagining hanging from trees high above the knolls and slopes of a forest. Or maybe she wasn't thinking at all.

Chapter 2

Trapped!

In the first class next day, everyone was seventy percent still asleep. Mr. Alister's idea of a fun lesson was to slowly flip the pages of his history text while students took turns reading aloud. The teacher had heard those chapters so many times he could be ninety percent still asleep, which he was right now.

Julie was reading page 114, paragraph two.

C. J. listened to her soft voice gliding smoothly over the words. He was determined to try to forget seven years of romantic hope. In his mind, he carved a new message into the bark of an imaginary tree: *Julie will love Raymond, not Wilson.*

But the round trunk of that tree deflated

like a punctured balloon. The message disappeared.

Maybe, if he delivered the love letter soon, his plan would work before it was too late.

Raymond was also listening to the history lesson singing through Julie's sweet voice. He tried to concentrate on the melody of the syllables, the way she read every line with confidence and emotion. But all he could think about was that Julie would probably be going to the dance with Wilson. And that might only be the beginning. It would take a miracle or a hurricane to change the way things were going.

* * *

"Julie. Ah . . . can I talk to you?"

The love letter C. J. had written the night before was safely hidden in his science book. But, standing there so close to Julie, he began to wonder what the heck he was doing helping Raymond win her heart.

Her dark brown hair was combed back into a curly ponytail with a red-velvet ribbon. Beautiful. And nobody had eyelashes as thick as Julie's. They were so long and turned up. And her brown eyes were so deep, so happy, so —

He shook his brain cells to get rid of those romantic thoughts and tried to focus on

Raymond who was about to give a love letter to Julie without even knowing it. C. J. knew he must now act purely in the name of friendship.

"Ah . . ."

"If you're going to start saying stupid stuff about Wilson asking me to the dance, C. J., you may as well forget it. You're just imagining things. Besides, someone told me he has a girlfriend in high school. So there."

"That doesn't mean anything. He might want two girlfriends. Or three. Who knows?"

"Look, C. J., I know we're friends, but that doesn't give you the right to —"

"I wasn't even going to mention Wilson."

"What did you want then?"

"Raymond . . . ah, he . . . ah, said to give you this." C. J. opened his science book to where he had folded his page of homework questions. "No. That's not it. Where did I . . . oh, here it is."

"What's this?"

"I dunno. Well, I sort of know. It's something Raymond wrote. Ah . . . he told me to give it to you. I didn't read it. I mean, if it's a letter or something like that, well, I didn't read it. I haven't a clue what's on that paper." He knew he'd better get out of there fast before his lies started to burn holes in his cheeks. "So, well, I'll see you in class."

Julie leaned against the wall and unfolded the letter:

Dear Julie,

For a long time I wanted to tell you about how I really like you a lot. That's why I'm writing this letter. If you want to, you can write me back.

With love,
from Raymond.

P.S. Maybe you would go to the dance with me on Thursday.

* * *

At noonhour, Raymond ate his sandwich in two chomps so he could escape from the crowded cafeteria to the safety of the library. In history class, he'd looked up to see three faces peering in through the narrow window of the classroom door. Three frowns. Three threats. Wilson, Terry, and Jay.

Noonhour was now almost over and Raymond was feeling less afraid. He'd found a corner in the library where no one noticed him working on his project about tropical fish. With only five minutes left, he gathered up his notes and headed to science class.

And there in the hall ambling along in their usual slow way were Wilson, Terry, and Jay. NIGHTMARE II!

"Hey! It's Knees!" yelled Terry.

"Where ya goin', Knees?" Wilson asked. "Stop and talk to your old pals, why don'tcha."

"Yea. Stop and talk to your pals," repeated Jay. He had a broad grin on his freckled face.

Standing there, surrounded by the grade nines, Raymond looked like a lonesome pine in the middle of a clump of briar bushes.

"Whatcha got there?" asked Wilson, trying to see the science project.

"Nothing."

"Looks like a project," said Terry.

"Then, it's like the guy said. He's got nothin'. A nothin' project. Ha Ha Ha."

The other two echoed Wilson's stupid laugh.

The taunting wafted up out of the briar bushes and floated down the hall just as Ms. Cameron emerged from her office.

Wilson had his hands on the corner of the science project. "Lemme see this nothing junk."

"Don't rip it!" Raymond released his grip on the precious pages.

"Fish? What's so scientific about fish? Fish stink. This project stinks!"

"Ha Ha Ha," chorused Jay and Terry.

Raymond's hopes of a high mark in science were sinking to the depths of a polluted sea.

"I guess I've seen enough of this game."

Suddenly no one was laughing.

"Return those papers immediately," said the vice-principal. "I'll have some company again in my office. We'll meet after school, this time. We shall place a few phone calls right now to advise your parents that you'll be arriving home at a later hour today."

Things might have been a lot different for Raymond if he'd walked away without looking back. But life just isn't that simple.

As the arrested grade nines followed Ms. Cameron to her office, Wilson sent a clear message to Raymond. It wasn't a message with actual words. It was, instead, a soundless snarl. For the second time this week, Ray could see his aunt's bulldog. Grrrrr. The difference was that each of these guys wasn't going to be on a leash for long.

Raymond's shoulders slumped with the weight of depression.

* * *

"That was weird," said Raymond to C. J. as they left science class and headed to French.

"What?"

"Something's weird about Julie."

"Julie? Something's weird about Julie?"

"Yea. Just now she gave me this strange look. All I said was hi."

"Strange look?"

Raymond stopped and looked down at C. J. "Why do you keep repeating what I say?"

"Repeating? I mean . . . Well, that's . . .

that's because I . . . I'm confused too. If you only said hi to her, I mean, what's the big deal? I haven't a clue why she'd give you a weird look."

Raymond glared at him. "I know you know something that I don't know. It's written all over your face."

"Bonjour," said Mme LeBlanc as she closed the classroom door behind her. "Comment allez-vous, aujourd'hui?"

C.J. slid into his desk, opened his notebook, and stared studiously at Mme LeBlanc. French. The language of love. It was the language of love that was getting him into deep trouble. He couldn't think of one single reason why he had written that love letter. His brain must have been on pause.

Raymond's mind was crammed with confusion too. Junior high school was turning into a torture chamber. Three grade nine thugs wouldn't leave him alone, and what had he done to them? Nothing! The girl he loved was obviously avoiding him and he didn't know why. And to top it all off, his best friend was trying to hide something from him. There were too many questions and not enough answers.

* * *

Everyone in 7S was silent. Everyone in 7S was writing. It was English class and, as usual, the first ten minutes were for writing. In his own journal, Mr. Saunders was deliberating upon a few dilemmas.

How did I ever get talked into having that critter as a class pet? It smells. I don't see the point of a hamster. It sleeps virtually all day. Now, here I am writing about that ball of rodent fur as if I don't have anything else on my mind.

I need a name for this stack of poems I hope will be a book some day. Pretentious thought. A book. Let's see . . . names, names, names. The Name of the Game. No, too much like a T.V. game show. Homeplate. No, too much like a recipe book.

Hey! I've got it! Extra Innings. I like that. Gives the sense of staying in the game. And what is poetry if not a game of words? I like it!

Back to reality. Thirty-two grade sevens.

There's got to be a better way to make a living.

"Put your journals away, please. C. J., you're up first. Let's reflect back on 'Casey at the Bat.' Tell the class what you concluded about the emotional state of our hero, Casey, when the second strike was called against him."

As Mr. Saunders hurriedly picked up his textbook, he created a waft of air across his desk, a zephyr which raised the top poem from the small stack there beside his journal. The page was lifted up as if by ghostly hands. It slipped over the edge of the desk and fluttered to the floor unnoticed.

* * *

After school, C. J. disappeared. It was a long walk home, but he didn't want to get cornered by Raymond asking more questions that would make him squirm with guilt. It was also a relief that he could avoid Julie. Avoid Julie! He never believed he'd have a thought like that in a million years!

Raymond didn't stop at the park, even though he knew the three grade nines were safely confined to the vice-principal's office. He just wasn't in the mood to daydream.

When he got home, he offered to make Amy's supper and feed her while his parents went for their daily walk. It was not a generous offer, actually. It was a selfish plan to get his father and mother out of the house so no one would ask questions about his down-in-the-dumps mood.

While his parents went for their walk, Raymond spooned turnip and carrot mush into Amy's tiny mouth. She squirted most of it back out again. It wasn't the most entertaining activity he could be doing, but Amy had a way of cheering him up. She blew vegetable bubbles and rocked in her high chair. Life for her was pretty simple.

* * *

The night custodian, Mrs. Warren, pushed her cart of cleaning supplies into Mr. Saunders' classroom and flicked on the lights. It was the last room she had to tidy before going home at eleven.

As she made her way around the room with a large mop, she stooped to pick up a science book, a pen, two pencils, a pair of sneakers, and, finally, a page of looseleaf. Since it wasn't crumpled, Mrs. Warren concluded that this paper was not meant for recycling. It had quite a nice poem about baseball on it, she noticed, although it didn't rhyme. Someone would be disappointed if they lost their hard work. She folded it carefully and placed it inside the math book that had been left on the nearest desk. That's likely the desk it fell from, she thought.

Resting her mop against the wall, she walked over to the small cage where Hobo was racing in her wheel. "You're in some awful rush to get somewhere, now aren't you, little fella? Where do you think that wheel's gonna take you?"

The hamster stopped her frantic race and came to the side of the cage, sniffing for freedom.

"Oh, aren't you the cutest thing, now. Let me just take you out so we can say hello."

The little legs ran foolishly in mid-air as Hobo was lifted out of her cage. Small bits of woodchips clung like lint to her fur coat.

"You want to play, do you? Well, there's no one here to play with except me and I'm going home in a few minutes. You'll have to wait until all the children come back in the morning. Yes, you will."

Hobo's small black eyes glanced furtively here and there. Tiny whiskers vibrated with the excitement of being out.

"Back you go to your little house. Back you go." She placed the wriggling body in the cage and gently shut the small latch. Too gently.

Click, and the lights were out.

Hobo sniffed and sniffed. She crept around to the wheel and sniffed again. She waddled over to her food dish, climbed inside, and munched three sunflower seeds. She sat and thought.

Then she went back to the wheel and thought again. Her mind was blank. She climbed up the side of the cage, poking her little pink nose out through the metal bars of the tiny door. Poke. Poke.

Before she could fill her blank mind with a clear idea, she heard a metallic sprrroong as the small latch popped open.

An hour later, as Mrs. Warren was sipping

tea with Mr. Warren, Hobo finished exploring all the small nooks and out-of-the-way places in Mr. Saunders' classroom. Then, she was curious about the shiny, clean, dark hallway.

As Hobo scurried and waddled and escaped down the empty hall, she sensed something new. Things weren't going to be the same as they had been in the confines of her hamster residence. Not one bit.

Scurry, waddle, wobble, waddle. Her furry bottom trailed small clouds of dust gathered from underneath a bookshelf. Hobo ventured on, instinctively searching for something nutritious, munchy, and delicious.

* * *

Miss Hiss was not quite asleep, and not quite awake. She wasn't famished, but a wish for food teased her tongue. In her imagination, there was a tiny scurrying sound. A little forest creature sound.

She had just been dreaming. In a dark wood, she had languished high on a sturdy branch, her elegant body wrapped around the rough bark. The intricate pattern on her leathery skin — brown, grey, and dusty beige — created a camouflage against the tree. A rustling sound below alerted her.

But there the dream had dissolved.

Sometimes, she was absolutely fed up with living inside her glass cage at the back of the science lab, waiting for the next handout. Was that any kind of life for a boa constrictor? Where was adventure? Where was the challenge of nourishment to be hunted down, cornered, and consumed?

Miss Hiss didn't even like her name.

Chapter 3

Empty Cages and Empty Pockets

"She's gone!" Julie stood beside the hamster cage. The small door was wide open. Inside, all was still: the wheel, the woodchips, the water dish. "Hobo's gone!!"

A half-hour of chaos followed that first shriek. Students were on their hands and knees peering under desks and radiators. Voices cooed and called in sounds meant to attract a wayward hamster. Small offerings of food were piled in places where a hungry Hobo might be hiding.

Suddenly Julie's voice pierced through the confusion. "AHHHHH!! The science lab! The boa constrictor! Oh, no!!"

"Let's not panic," said Mr. Saunders. "If the

team doesn't stay cool, calm, and collected, there'll be no hope of success in this game. That snake is safely under glass. The science lab is in another wing of this building. These are the facts!"

As the news spread throughout the school, everyone offered to help find Hobo.

Coach Willis ordered his whole gym class to peer into places where a hamster might choose to snooze. They opened every locker. They sorted through the floor hockey sticks, volleyballs, basketballs, and boxes of nets.

Mrs. Francis, the school secretary, did her best to search for the hamster throughout the office, even though she hoped with all her heart that she wouldn't be the one to find it.

Mr. Saunders and Ms. Harrison were seen on their hands and knees in the copy room, their cheeks on the floor, straining to see under the photocopier.

"How can you possibly tell a hamster from a dustball?" Mr. Sanders remarked in frustration.

Ms. Harrison delicately lifted a clump of dust from his sweater.

Mr. Grant, the health teacher, muttered something under his breath about rodents and disinfectant.

Wilson, Terry, and Jay made jokes about hamster roadkill and lifted their feet as though to check for a flattened body on the bottoms of their large sneakers. A few people even laughed at their sick humor.

The vice-principal announced a hamster alert to the whole school just before recess began.

But even after all the searching, Hobo was nowhere to be found. The cage was still empty at the front of the classroom.

Ms. Harrison reassured 7S that the boa constrictor posed not a thread of a threat. But no one believed that Hobo was out of danger. Wherever she was.

* * *

The line-up for dance tickets was moving slowly, and Raymond was third from the last. Ordinarily, he wouldn't have minded just standing around. He could listen to what people were saying or watch what they were doing. But this time, Wilson, Terry, and Jay were leaning against the wall looking right at him and saying stuff he couldn't hear. It made him very, very nervous.

Finally, he was at the front of the line. He bought his dance ticket (only one) and rushed off to the library. Three sinister pairs of eyes followed him.

He hurried into the book stacks, out of sight.

"Hey, Knees. How come you're hiding here behind all these stupid books?"

Wilson, Terry, and Jay crammed into the small space and moved toward him.

"I'm not hiding."

"Looks like it to us, doesn't it, guys?" said Wilson.

His two goons nodded and grinned.

"Maybe he's got something? Like money, maybe?" Wilson held out his hand. "We know you got money, Knees, because we just saw you pay for a dance ticket. Looked like you got money back. Me and my friends sure could use some money, couldn't we, guys?"

Terry and Jay grinned even more.

"I'm not giving it to you." Raymond tried to make his voice sound unafraid.

"We say you *are* going to give it to us. Or else you might just have a surprise today on your way home from school. Such as in that park where you go when there's no one else around." Wilson slid his fist back and forth on his palm, as if he were polishing a deadly weapon.

Raymond looked quickly at Terry. He must've told his pals he'd seen Raymond there the other day. The park would be a perfect place for final revenge. In his mind, Raymond could hear a loud SNAP! Then another, and another. Like the sound of three leashes snapping as three bulldogs broke free.

He reached reluctantly into his jeans pocket and took out all his money, four dollars and fifty cents. Wilson grabbed it.

"Hey," said Terry. "What about the dance ticket?"

Wilson snarled and held out his hand again. Raymond put the dance ticket into Wilson's grubby paw.

"Boys? Is there something I can help you find?"

At the sound of the librarian's voice, Raymond felt a rush of relief. But it was too late; his pockets were now empty.

"Naw. We were just looking around," said Wilson.

Raymond didn't say a word. He knew if he didn't keep his mouth shut, he might find himself lying unconscious in the leaves beside the river.

He avoided the puzzled stare of the librarian and left, keeping a safe distance behind Wilson, Terry, and Jay.

A new feeling seeped like poison into his brain: Raymond felt ashamed. Okay, so those grade nine guys had been harrassing him for days. It was bad enough they were getting away with that. But now they were stealing from him. And he had let them do it. He had just wimpered there like a mouse. What kind of a guy was he turning into? A beanpole with no guts!

* * *

It was 2:45. Hobo was still lost.

"Look," said Mr. Saunders, firmly. "There is no need for this air of gloom and doom. The game's not over yet. We've only played a couple innings."

"If we don't find Hobo soon, something awful will happen. I just know it," wailed Julie.

Raymond sat with his cheek resting on his hand. He heard the pain in Julie's voice, but he had no room in his heart for her sadness or for Hobo's predicament. Come to think of it, he'd trade places with that miniature creature in a minute. Anything would be better than being who he was: Raymond the Chicken-heart.

"The hamster will be all right," said Mr. Saunders. "You've scattered enough food for it to feed on. Tonight, it will probably skitter out of its hiding place and Mrs. Warren will find it. They're nocturnal creatures, after all."

"What if Hobo roams down to the science lab?" moaned Julie.

"Ms. Harrison says there's no doubt the snake is secure in its cage."

Once again, no one was reassured.

* * *

That night, Raymond offered to read Amy a bedtime story. His parents would likely ask him their usual question if he hung around watching T.V. or doing his homework at the kitchen table: How was school today, Raymond? Oh, fine. Just fine. Yep. Fine, fine, fine. He'd be ashamed to admit that he'd actually given money and a dance ticket to three thugs.

Amy lay in her crib and listened to the sound of Raymond's voice. He usually didn't read Amy's books to her. Bunnies and bears didn't interest him much. So he was reading a novel about dwarfs and giants, telepathic visions and supernatural strength. Amy seemed to like the action scenes best.

Just before he went to bed, he turned his piggybank upside down and shook it until enough money rattled out to pay for a dance ticket. Again.

* * *

C. J. sat at the small desk in his bedroom and hauled the math book out of his backpack. Homework. Yuk! Math teachers must think the brain is an empty can waiting to be filled to the brim with math trash: fractions, whole numbers, integers, formulas, blah, blah, blah.

He flipped open the book. What's this? A neatly folded piece of paper. He didn't remember putting any looseleaf inside his math book.

A poem?

C. J. read it carefully. It was quite a long poem. About baseball. Where did it come from? Who'd write a poem about baseball? And it didn't even rhyme. It wasn't as good as "Casey at the Bat" but —

Then it hit him! The person who would write such a long poem about baseball had to be a baseball freak — Mr. Saunders! He couldn't believe it. Mr. Saunders was a poet! But how could one of his teacher's poems end up in this math book?

Suddenly, C. J. dropped the paper as if it were on fire. Would Mr. Saunders think he had stolen it?

Somehow, he'd have to get it back on Mr. Saunder's desk without anyone knowing.

* * *

Julie was sitting on the windowseat in her bedroom, staring out into the darkness, worrying.

First, there was Hobo. Where was the tiny hamster right now? Shivering in some shadowy corner of that vast and empty school? When she tried to picture Hobo happily munching on some carrot sticks, she saw a horrifying image of a coiled boa constrictor ready to strike.

Then there was that strange note C. J. had delivered. *With love, from Raymond.* Deep in her heart, she knew she would have to stand face to face with Raymond and let him know that her feelings for him weren't the same as his feelings for her. That was going to be tough.

Then there was Wilson. Everybody said that he wasn't the kind of guy a girl should be seen with. He swore all the time. He smoked cigarettes. Someone said he got kicked out of a dance when he was in grade eight because he started a fight. And someone else said that Wilson had no mother, that she'd walked out on them, that it was just him and his father and a stepbrother who lived at their house. She knew for a fact that the police had gone to Wilson's place once last summer. Her own mother's friend had seen the police car there.

But when he talked to her, Wilson was always nice. And he smelled good too, sort of a peppery smell from aftershave. His eyes were kind of melty, and he had a warm smile. She liked how he was tall, how, when she stood beside him, her nose was at the height of his shoulder.

She wished he didn't hang around those other two guys so much. When he was away from them, Wilson acted more like an ordinary, nice guy.

* * *

Mr. Saunders leaned over a scribbled page. His fist curled around a clump of his hair as he concentrated. He had been unable to remember all of the words of his lost poem. It still didn't sound right. How could he ever recover the work of hours and hours of thinking and rethinking, deciding and undeciding? Why had he thrown away all those drafts?

Just before he turned off his bedside light, Mr. Saunders had a very strange image flash across his mind. He saw a small, furry creature huddled in a dusty corner of the classroom, munching a large hole through the center of the baseball poem.

* * *

Under a sofa in the teachers' room sat Hobo, too full of crackers to find room in her pouch for this newly found morsel — a peanut. She scratched at the fraying carpet to make a small hole, and then tucked the peanut against the tangled threads. Later, she would enjoy this tantalizing treat.

* * *

Miss Hiss was dreaming. There was a thick tree tangled with vines in the midst of a hot, damp jungle. A butterfly fluttered by and then perched on a leaf. Its delicate saffron wings stirred in the gentle afternoon breeze. Miss Hiss appreciated the beauty of nature.

She hung her head lazily over the limb

around which her long body was wrapped. The sunbeams made intricate patterns on the jungle floor, a dancing puzzle of shadow and light. Ahhh, life in the wild was —

Suddenly, the snake was shaken from her sleep.

Where . . .?

What . . .?

She squinted into the darkness. The jungle images had disappeared. Life in the wild was not the life which Miss Hiss was living.

She sighed. The sigh rippled slowly down the long length of her graceful body the way a wave moves in a pond when the smallest leaf falls on its quiet surface.

* * *

Before dawn, Hobo had found refuge underneath the photocopier in the library. She curled into a replica of a dustball and fell asleep.

Chapter 4

Dance 'til You Drop!

Raymond tucked his shirt in. Then he pulled it out and stood back from the mirror. Yes. Not so dressed-up looking. But the color was wrong. Green made him look gawky, like the Jolly Green Giant.

He went back to his closet and searched for something red. Red made him look regal, like a Royal Canadian Mounted Police.

* * *

C. J. squeezed gel out of the tube and rubbed his hands together. Then he leaned toward the bathroom mirror, spreading his greasy palms smoothly over his head. He carved an even part in the middle of his hair and combed it straight down each side.

The person peering out at him from the mirror looked like a mobster about to bump off a rival gang leader.

He put his head under the tap and washed his hair for the third time.

Next to the dance ticket on C. J.'s bureau lay Mr. Saunder's baseball poem. Maybe tonight, when everyone was in the gym and the classrooms were dark, he would have an opportunity to plant that poem in a place where his teacher would find it.

* * *

Wilson, Terry, and Jay were standing together beside Max's Quik-Mart. Terry was handing out cigarettes that he'd stolen from his grandfather's pack as the old man snoozed in front of the T.V. Jay had just bought a new lighter and was trying to get it to work.

"Lemme see that thing," said Wilson impatiently. He flicked and flicked but no flame appeared.

"It's baby-proof," said Terry, which might not have been the best thing for him to say to Wilson.

"Yea," said Jay. "You gotta use two hands."

"I knew that, you idiots!" Wilson flicked.

And flicked again. Finally, they had flame, and cigarettes were lit all around.

* * *

Julie took the blue ribbon out of her ponytail and brushed her hair again. She sighed. It was hard to get into a dance mood.

For two nights and three whole days, Hobo had been missing. None of the food they'd left in the classroom had been touched. However, some crackers left in the hallway had hamster-sized bites out of them. She hoped with all her heart that Mr. Saunders was right about how Hobo could take care of herself.

Then Julie had a really cheerful thought: maybe they'd find Hobo tonight, during the dance! After all, hamsters were night creatures, weren't they? Right!

She brushed her hair again. It was long, almost to her shoulders, and the curls fell soft and brown around her face. When her hair wasn't tied back in a ponytail, Julie looked different. Older. Maybe she wouldn't wear her hair in a ponytail tonight.

She smiled into the mirror as though someone had just asked her to dance and she was saying yes.

* * *

Mr. Saunders washed his dishes (one plate, one knife, one fork, two spoons, a small pot, and a coffee cup) and stacked them in the drainer to dry. He rinsed out the empty can (Rancher's Beans 'n Pork), then tossed it into the recycling bag.

He looked around the small space of his bachelor apartment with a frown. Where could it be? He had searched everywhere. It was the best poem in his collection and his attempts to rewrite it had failed.

Well, he decided, he'd search once again through his desk at school. That's where he'd seen it last. Since he was obliged to chaperone at the dance (an activity which he found most unpoetic), he could do it that night. He'd also organize another search party for the roaming rodent. The thought of yet another whole day of students grieving over their absent class pet was unbearable.

Before turning off the lights and shutting the door of his apartment, Mr. Saunders gazed longingly at the sharpened pencils and smooth, new writing paper. They'd have to wait. The Muses did not attend junior high school dances.

* * *

Julie arrived wearing a yellow blouse, a short black skirt, black stockings and black boots.

Her hair fell in loose curls to her shouders. She went immediately to the 7S classroom and looked for Hobo in every nook and cranny. No luck.

C. J. gave his ticket at the door and rushed to the washroom to see if the gel still held his hair in place (a side part with one curl on his forehead). He double-checked to be sure the baseball poem was in the back pocket of his jeans. As soon as he could, he'd sneak down to the classroom and finally get rid of it.

Raymond was handsome in his father's red sweater and his own new black jeans. When he saw Julie coming out of their classroom, he offered to help search for Hobo. Together, they investigated that wing of the school. No luck. And another sign that this might not be his lucky night was that Julie was still acting weird. You'd think he had pizza sauce smeared all over his face.

Wilson, Terry, and Jay strolled in together with the stagnant smell of cigarettes on their breath.

When Mr. Saunders arrived, Ms. Harrison tactfully told him he had a gooey stain on his tie. He went into the staff room to clean off the footprint of one brown bean. Then, he went to his classroom to rifle once more through his desk for the missing poem. No luck.

Before the excitement of the dance consumed everyone's energy, Mr. Saunders formed a posse of students to carry out a search for Hobo through the entire building. They made so much racket he was sure the critter would cower fearfully away from them, somewhere safe.

The gymnasium was soon a circus of gyrating bodies. From the electric eyes of the lighting equipment on stage, colors of blue, red, and green pulsed into the crowd. An eerie haze from the smoke machine hung in the air. Sound slammed into the walls and bounced off the floor and the ceiling. It vibrated the blood cells in everyone's veins: the dancers, the chaperones, the custodian, and the tiny, hidden hamster that stared out, wide-eyed, from a small hole under the stage.

Haliburton Junior High was rockin'!!

Raymond was watching Julie. C. J. was watching Raymond watching Julie.

Wilson had his eye on Julie, too. He and Jay and Terry ambled around the perimeter of the gymnasium as if they were strolling in a park, unaware of the animal life surrounding them. Very cool.

The DJ announced the second waltz like this: "Okay, everybody. Let's slow things down a bit here so you can get close to your heart's desire."

A small crowd of people left the gymnasium like the rush of shoppers when the mall closes. This was not because they didn't have a heart's desire, but because they didn't want to be left standing alone if their heart's desire didn't desire them.

Raymond walked toward Julie.

Wilson deserted Terry and Jay. He made a path through the dancers leading directly to Julie.

Raymond got there first. He asked Julie to dance and she said yes.

Wilson almost stopped in his tracks. But that wouldn't be cool. So he continued carving a path through the waltzing couples, until he was standing in the doorway leading into the gym. His narrow eyes strained through the red and blue lights to see Raymond with Julie. His narrow mind planned revenge.

When the waltz was over, Raymond looked down at Julie and tried on a smile that said something like: *Thanks for the dance. I'd like to ask you again. Maybe we'll even have the last waltz.*

Julie was thinking that Raymond's smile said something like: *I love you now and forever. Maybe we should go steady and then get married some day.*

So she looked way up into his green eyes and said very softly, "I like you, Raymond. But like a friend. Not like you like me."

He was stunned! How did she know he liked her? He felt as if his mind was a glass bowl and his thoughts were bright goldfish swimming inside. He panicked.

When he got to the door of the gymnasium, he didn't see Wilson standing there. The DJ had just popped another disk into the machine — the most popular Jumping-Jacks' hit — and suddenly the door was jammed with dancers bolting back into the gym.

As Raymond rushed past, Wilson quickly raised his arms like he was stretching, timing it perfectly so his fist would collide with Raymond's eye. It happened so slickly that no one actually saw it happen, least of all Raymond whose left eye was suddenly slammed shut. Wilson smoothly disappeared into the darkness of the dance.

Mr. Saunders held an ice pack against Raymond's left eye. "You've got a shiner there, but I can see no real damage to the eye. You'll be back on the batter's mound before the next inning."

C.J. rushed into the office. "Hey, Ray. What happened? I just heard someone punched you in the eye!"

"Rumors, C. J.," muttered Mr. Saunders. "They fly through the crowd like foul balls — worthless. Your friend, here, seems to have been a victim of the modern dance. All that flailing of arms is bound to result in minor injury."

"You going home?" asked C. J.

"Yea. They called Dad to come get me."

"I could go with you. If you want."

"I'm all right. No sense you missing the dance too."

An hour and a half later, when the last waltz was announced, C. J. stood in the shadow of the amplifiers near the equipment-room door and watched Wilson ask Julie to dance. He fumed as Wilson's grade-nine arms wrapped around Julie's small body. He cringed as Wilson's face rested romantically against the soft, brown curls of Julie's beautiful hair. He died inside as he realized that the best-laid plans of mice and men do often go astray. His love letter from Raymond had obviously failed.

Behind C. J.'s right foot, where blue and green light leaked in through the hole under the stage, Hobo trembled. Her hopes for a night of scurrying and waddling through the dark expanse of the empty school had somehow been shattered by light, sound, and bouncing teenagers. Hamsters, like mice and men, can't rely on plans they make either.

* * *

Midnight. Thursday was turning into Friday as Hobo scampered down the hallway, her belly dusting the floor along the way. Sniff. Sniff. Sniff. She investigated every nook for that peanut. Where had she hidden it?

* * *

In the science lab, Miss Hiss slithered
the entire length of herself, stretching and
stretching and stretching. She stretched so far
even she was surprised. Farther even than she
had earlier that day when Ms. Harrison had
taken her out of the cage to show off her
perfectly patterned boa body.

Sssshe ssssstretched even farther.

Miss Hiss was, in fact, out of the cage. She
was stretching, slithering, sliding, curving
along the floor. Ms. Harrison, for the first (and
last) time, had not been extra, extra careful
when she had placed her precious pet back in
its pen.

Now, with a soft moan, the door of the
science lab opened just wide enough for
the thick and rippling width of a boa constrictor to pass through. Miss Hiss continued
down the hallway in search of warmth. And
possibly food.

* * *

Wilson was walking alone because Terry and
Jay lived over by the school and he lived back
behind the mall in a new subdivision. Some
brainwave architect figured it would disguise
the fact that every single house was exactly
the same if they were painted different colors

and if the front doors had different shaped windows. Only idiots would be fooled.

This is what Wilson was thinking about as he approached his own house (pale blue with a crescent-shaped window in the front door). He flicked his cigarette into the gutter and started up the walkway. That's when he got the feeling, the same one every time. It felt as if his stomach had turned into a spinning tire and his heart raced into overdrive.

His stepbrother's car was parked in the driveway. This was odd because Jason hardly ever came home until it was just about time for breakfast. The vice-principal at his school had their phone number memorized, he'd called so many times when Jason didn't show up for school.

Wilson was relieved when he saw that no one was downstairs in the kitchen or watching T.V. in the den. When he went upstairs, he saw that Jason's bedroom door was shut. So was his father's. Making as little noise as possible, he softly shut his own bedroom door, got undressed and climbed into bed. Maybe tonight he'd get to sleep right through until dawn.

* * *

C. J. had peeled off his jeans and dumped them on the floor beside his bed. He was exhausted. And he was thinking about Raymond's eye. *It's probably swelled up like a purple jellyfish by now. Man, that must've hurt. Weird how no one said that it was their fist that did it. It wasn't like they'd get in trouble or anything because of how it was an accident. And how could someone's fist land in another person's eye and they wouldn't know it happened? Weird.*

These thoughts had crowded C. J.'s mind, leaving no room for him to remember the piece of looseleaf which was still tucked into the back pocket of his jeans. And, the next morning, when C. J.'s father shouted upstairs for him to bring his dirty clothes down to the laundry room, his mind was too clogged with sleep to remember Mr. Saunders' baseball poem.

It was luck (and it wasn't luck) that his father always checked pockets before starting the wash. If it had been C. J.'s turn to do the laundry, the poem would have been converted into paper paste.

When his dad unfolded the looseleaf, he was pleasantly surprised to find a fairly well-written poem about baseball. It didn't rhyme, but it wasn't bad. Not bad at all.

C. J.'s handwriting was atrocious, though, so his dad decided to type it on the computer for him. He used a nice bold font, and then added a baseball graphic which made the poem look quite professional.

That's when a brilliant idea occurred to him. He remembered seeing a full-page ad in the newspaper just the other day. A poetry contest was being held by their local cable television station. He decided that C. J.'s poem, "Outfielder's Dreams," should be sent in to this competition. Wouldn't C. J. be surprised if he actually won!!

Chapter 5

Attack!

The sun rose through thick purple clouds, splashing orange against the windows of Haliburton Junior High and throwing narrow beams like searchlights into classrooms.

The light fell upon a scurrying hamster that paused, alert, its tiny feet splayed on shiny tile, ready for escape. Sensing no danger in the warm, silent light, Hobo continued her search for a safe, dark corner in which to sleep all day.

The sunrise beamed into the home economics lab and sparkled on the chrome taps and polished counters. From above, where the heating pipes crisscrossed the ceiling, two sleepy eyes looked down at the patterns of light. An ancient memory stirred in the snake's brain: a summer stream sliding below, catching the morning rays and tossing them like jewels into the air. Her long body was wrapped contentedly around the warmth of a dusty, insulated heating pipe.

Before long, the two creatures were sound asleep not even ten yards apart. Hobo had squeezed into a hole behind a radiator in the hallway. And there she'd found another small opening leading into a cozy cupboard with pots, pans and cooling racks stacked like castle walls to hide behind.

It would be a few hours before Miss Hiss would hear the rattle of a pot cover, then the distinct sound of scampering and woolly wabbling.

Outside, purple clouds had thickened to ominous grey and pushed the sun out of sight.

Raymond let his mother drive him to school. She had told him he could stay home if he felt self-conscious about his eye. But he'd decided to get it over with. People were going to stare. People were going to hound him with questions. Waiting until Monday wouldn't do much good because that eye was going to look like baked eggplant for a long time.

But when Raymond entered the school, no one paid him even the slightest attention. Chaos and confusion had turned the world of Haliburton Junior High upside down! People were cowering in clusters, wimpering or wailing. "The boa constrictor has escaped! Miss Hiss is out!"

Ms. Harrison was wringing her hands and assuring everyone that her pet wasn't dangerous. But they all remembered what she'd said earlier that week. Now, this snake that would never get out of its glass cage was out. So there was no doubt that the reptile would live up to its reputation — someone was going to be the victim of a boa embrace.

The first person Raymond actually focused on in all the mayhem was Julie, and she was sobbing. "Oh, Raymond. What'll we do? The snake's gonna get Hobo! I just know it!"

He put his hand on her shoulder and tried to say something comforting. "Hobo's probably nowhere near where the boa is right now. This school's got so many hiding places for a hamster. And that boa's so big. They'll find it before the first bell rings, I bet."

Just then, like a death knell, the first bell rang and students began to make their way cautiously to classes.

When the first group bustled into the home economics lab, no one was looking up. The teacher handed out papers for a test, reassuring the students that a team of searchers was scouring the school. "That snake is probably hiding somewhere away from the light of day. Somewhere damp, such as the basement. I'm sure boa constrictors like cool, damp, dark spaces."

Mr. Saunders was the first person to remark on Raymond's eye, but he wasn't entirely telling the truth. "Well, well, your eye doesn't look half bad actually. I once saw a World Series game. Night game. Braves against the Jays. Jays lost in the eleventh inning. Anyway, the first baseman collided with the pitcher trying to catch a fly ball. Now that was a shiner. The pitcher's eye looked like a catcher's mitt. Couldn't play ball for a week."

A small sob turned Mr. Saunders' attention away from his baseball memory to the third seat in row five where Julie had her head down on her desk.

"It's Hobo," said C.J. "Julie's worried. Because of how he's not the only thing missing in this school right now."

Mr. Saunders tried to paste a casual smile on his face to hide the image which slipped morbidly into his mind: a slithering snake cornering a horrified hamster.

"Not to worry. Not to worry," he said. "It's one thing for a tiny hamster to be missing. But how long could a twelve-foot boa constrictor with a girth bigger than a baseball bat stay lost?"

At the detailed description of the size of the snake, Julie sobbed even louder.

This day was going to be one of longest Fridays of his ten-year teaching career. Mr. Saunders gazed over the heads of the students and watched the dark clouds drift drearily by his classroom window.

In the home economics lab, all was quiet as the students wrote the fill-in-the-blank test. Their teacher strolled up and down the aisles. She was just about to announce that five minutes were left, when, from a nearby cupboard, came the familiar sound of a pot cover rattling. Odd. Convincing herself and the class that a boa constrictor couldn't possibly get into a closed cupboard, she went over to investigate.

High above, hugging the warmth of the heating pipes, Miss Hiss awoke. A rattle? Tiny toenail sounds of a rodent stirring? Lunch?

When the teacher slowly opened the cupboard door, she found nothing, much to her intense relief and, of course, to the relief of the twenty-six pairs of fearful eyes that followed her every move.

Hobo no longer inhabited that cupboard. She was now snugly tucked into the small space between the walls, near the heat of the radiator.

"Sometimes pots will just slide," the teacher explained to her class, "especially if they haven't been stacked properly." Maybe she would've given another keep-your-kitchen-clean lecture if the bell hadn't rung at that very moment. "Pass in your tests, please, as you leave the room!"

For the third time that week, a door that should have been closed was left slightly ajar as the teacher collected her fill-in-the-blank tests. A draft seeped in past the pots, pans, and cooling racks to where Hobo hid between the walls.

Miss Hiss gazed down at the tops of all those heads leaving the room. Her keen eyes studied the door of the cupboard from where she'd heard the scurrying sounds.

The teacher then sat at her desk to mark tests. Next period no class was scheduled in the home economics lab. She could enjoy some peace and quiet. But just as she put her red marking pen down on the first paper, she had an unusual feeling. Was she being watched?

She turned her head to the right and looked out the three windows. No one there. She turned her head to the left and surveyed the kitchen area. Empty. The desks were also unoccupied. No one stood at the window of the classroom door. Shaking off that unreasonable feeling, the tired teacher resumed her marking.

Miss Hiss watched the quick, quick movements of the pen — check, check, check, X — down the pages of the fill-in-the-blank tests. It mesmerized her.

* * *

At recess, Julie was being really nice to Raymond, especially considering she had so much on her mind. He was starting to wonder if she was having second thoughts about him. In fact, she even bought him a bag of chips.

Actually, Julie was feeling guilty. She had no reason to be, no reason at all. But somehow she got it into her head that she should help Raymond feel better about having his eye bashed by accident when she couldn't make him feel better about having his heart squished by rejection.

Terry and Jay were following Wilson around as usual, wondering why they weren't harassing Knees today. That purple smear across his eye was perfect bait for taunting. But it was easier to let Wilson do all the planning and deciding.

And Wilson was doing just that.

He didn't like the fact that Julie was pampering Raymond like he was some kind of invalid and she was a private nurse. It was making Wilson burn — a smoldering burn. There wasn't much time before it would flash into angry fire.

C. J. asked Raymond if he wanted to just hang out in the gym at lunch hour. Outside, it was pelting rain. Maybe it would even thunder. Charcoal clouds were making the day like night.

Everyone was forced to stay in the gymnasium or in the entrance hall because of the snake alert. Ms. Harrison was leading her search party in a methodical way throughout the building. They had moved from the science lab through the entire west wing and into the north wing where the boiler room seemed the most likely hiding place. No luck. Now they were almost finished the east wing. Just the art room and the home economics lab left.

The boys' volleyball team was playing an exhibition game against the girls' team. Julie had volunteered to referee, hoping that the job would preoccupy her anguished mind.

C. J. and Raymond leaned against the stage just behind the chair where Julie stood. With his one good eye, Raymond watched her head follow the action of the game: left, right, left, up. She blew the whistle as the ball hit the rafters.

Wilson, Terry, and Jay were standing in the entrance to the gym. Actually, it was the exact same place Wilson had stood when Raymond had waltzed with Julie the night before. Now he was watching as Raymond oggled Julie. The smoldering in his brain heated closer to the igniting point.

"Let's go," Wilson said to Terry and Jay. The authority in his voice told them something serious was up. He bulldozed a path through the spectators toward the stage. The way he moved, you'd think there was a fire.

Raymond might've seen Wilson coming if his left eye hadn't been swollen shut. C.J. was on Raymond's right-hand side, and he was following the volleyball which sailed up, up over the net and arched to the back line of the court.

Julie studied the ball to be sure of the precise place it landed. Inside! Point! She blew the whistle in a quick, shrill blast.

That's when Wilson's shoulder slammed into Raymond like a truck colliding with a cardboard box. Raymond's tall, thin body spun out from the stage, fell sideways against the chair where Julie stood, and tumbled to the floor. His head connected with the volleyball net pole. Then everything went still.

If snapshots had been taken, they would have revealed so much detail in that split-second of time.

Wilson had the faintest smile of satisfaction on his face. He'd made a clean hit, for sure. A second later his expression changed to the one he used hundreds of times: a gaping mouth to convince people of how surprised he was. It seemed to say: Geez, how did that happen?!

The picture of C. J. would have only shown the back of his head because it took him more than five seconds to realize that the commotion beside him was Raymond falling down.

Julie lost her balance when Raymond's

body hit the back of her chair; so in the photo-graph, she would have been in mid-air. She had no way of knowing what had happened behind her.

Two teachers were suddenly beside Raymond's still body, checking his breathing, lifting his hand, shouting for an ambulance. Another teacher pushed back the crowd that had moved in.

In that crowd was Wilson. His face was sculptured to show no feeling at all, but his heart was racing. *I just pushed the guy a little, that's all. How'd I know he was gonna fall? How could I help it if the stupid pole was right there? How?*

C. J. couldn't move. He felt his brain numbing and his stomach oozing fear. Raymond was lying there on the floor. His head was resting sideways as if he were asleep. One arm lay across his chest and the other out by his side, his hand slightly cupped as if he expected someone to pass him some-thing fragile.

The siren of the ambulance frightened everyone. It wailed up the driveway and groaned to a stop in front of the school. The paramedics ran with metal boxes and kitbags and a stretcher, their faces stiff, their minds focused on all the rules they had in their heads.

In seconds, Raymond was on the stretcher. His face was covered by an oxygen mask as one attendant leaned over him, running sideways, saying his name: Raymond, Raymond, Raymond.

There was no time to ask how or why.

Chapter 6

Hope

The hospital emergency department was quiet and still. One patient, holding gauze against the tip of his finger, waited to get stitches. The nurse on duty was filling out a requisition form for more requisition forms.

Everything was clean and white: the walls, the floors, the counters, the nurse's starched uniform and his shoes. The clock on the wall showed the passing seconds with a constant but silent movement of electric hands.

Then, from a block away, the panic wail of an ambulance could be heard. The emergency department came alive. Two more nurses appeared from a back office as a doctor rushed into the room.

The ambulance pulled up to the double doors. Gadgets were mounted in place. The doctor checked Raymond's vital signs as she ran along beside the stretcher.

A small blue car screeched to a stop. Raymond's parents hurried into the emergency department, finally beside their son, holding his hand, smoothing his hair, not thinking, not believing, only hoping and hoping and hoping.

* * *

C. J. and Julie sat in the deserted stairwell at school. They were both thinking so hard they could find nothing to say. Raymond. Will he be okay? Are his eyes open? Can he think? Can he talk? How bad is he?

"There you are." Mr. Saunders stood at the top of the stairs. "You guys okay?"

"Yea. Well, sort of," said C. J.

"Want to talk?"

"No thanks, sir." C. J. felt a bit stupid saying that, as if Mr. Saunders were passing out candies and he could just politely say no. "But thanks for asking anyway." That sounded even more stupid. Nothing was coming out right.

Julie looked up. She started to smile but then looked down at her sneakers.

"Raymond's going to be fine," said Mr.

Saunders. "His parents just called. They said the doctors are doing everything they can."

Everything they can. That was too much like a line in all the worst movies when everyone knows there's no hope. Mr. Sauders turned around and went back to his classroom, hoping C. J. and Julie could make it through this thing together.

"You think Ray's gonna die?" As soon as the words were out, C. J. wished he could gobble them back up. Die? Raymond? Wasn't it impossible?

Julie hugged her knees and rocked.

"I mean, I don't think he's gonna die or anything like that. I . . . I just wondered, like, if that's what you were thinking. If that's why you were crying, I mean."

"I'm just afraid, that's all," she said. The way her voice quivered made C. J. look away.

His heart gave a small lurch again. Those images of Raymond wouldn't go away: his eyes closed, his face so white except for that swollen purple patch, his hand just lying there sort of open beside him. And the stretcher. And the paramedics saying Raymond's name over and over again as if he had gone somewhere else and had left his body behind.

"It's just that . . . well, that note he wrote to me? The one he asked you to give to me?" said Julie. "He said stuff and, well, I just wish I could say something back to him."

At the reminder of the love letter he'd written to Julie from Raymond, C. J. squirmed. It seemed so stupid now. More than stupid. Who'd he think he was anyway, acting like he could just write anything he wanted and sign Raymond's name and then give it to Julie? As if he could take over Raymond's life, like he was some kind of god or something.

"I mean, if something happens to Raymond . . . what I mean is, I'd like to tell him how much I like him. Which is a lot. But not . . . Well, in that letter, he said stuff about . . . about that he loved me. And, well, I don't love him. But, I mean, I love him but not in that way that he was talking about in the letter." She let tears slide down her cheeks without wiping them away.

C. J. couldn't speak. Now his lie was spreading further.

"I think if someone loves you, not just likes you but loves you, then it's really an honor," said Julie. "I mean, they kind of are putting you up in a special place. Like Raymond did. He put me in a special place and no one ever did that before. I mean, my parents do and Nan and Graw do, but not like a boyfriend, I mean."

C. J. felt an odd sensation of jealousy. Julie would never say those things about him, especially if she knew the truth about what kind of a guy he really was. The kind of guy who acted like he owned another guy's life. The kind of guy who could be jealous of his best friend even when his best friend was in a coma.

"Ever since I can remember, Raymond's been a really nice person. Someone you could count on," Julie was saying. "Who wouldn't lie or get mad. Not really mad, anyway. That's what I mean about how it's an honor. Not like with Wilson. He says things and you know it's just words falling out of his mouth. If Raymond says he loves a person, then he does."

"And I think he does, too," said C. J. "Like if he could say it himself, he would."

For a moment, Julie wasn't quite sure what C. J. was talking about. "Like out loud, you mean?"

Even though the lie was burrowing deeper, this wasn't the time to reveal the whole truth. "Yea. Not just in a letter."

"If I live to be a hundred, I bet no boy who ever loves me will be better than Raymond."

"If I live to be a hundred, I won't ever have a better best friend either."

* * *

Terry and Jay stood beside Wilson at the window of the boys' washroom, smoking a cigarette, passing it from one set of yellow fingers to the next.

"What if he dies?" Terry said, exhaling through the opened window. "He looked pretty bad."

"Don't be stupid." Wilson grabbed the stub of cigarette and inhaled. His eyes checked the door, the schoolyard, the ash at the end of the cigarette. "You're really stupid, you know that?"

Jay was slouched against the radiator, nervously biting his thumbnail and waiting to get a drag on the cigarette. Wilson inhaled a couple more times and then dropped the butt to the floor and stepped on it.

"Maybe Terry's right," Jay said. "I heard his head when it hit that pole. Geez, it made some awful sound. Like his skull just split. Like bone cracking wide open."

"You been watching too many movies, you dummy," said Wilson.

"I'm no dummy," Jay said. "I wasn't the one who hit him."

"What's that supposed to mean?"

"Just what it says."

Terry had moved to stand beside Jay.

Wilson faced them both. Something felt different. Like quicksand. "No one hit him," he said angrily.

"Right. Until someone starts asking questions," said Jay. "You think I'm gonna say I hit him? No way. I think we otta tell the truth.

They can't prove you meant it anyways. We could say it was an accident."

"It was an accident. What're you talking about? Besides, maybe one of you guys bumped into me and I lost my balance. Maybe you did it on purpose? Who's gonna say you didn't?"

Jay started to nervously bite his thumbnail again. Terry looked down at the floor, losing confidence.

That quicksand feeling was suddenly gone and Wilson knew for certain that Jay and Terry would keep their mouths shut. Or else.

* * *

Over Raymond's face was the clear plastic of the oxygen mask. On the finger of his right hand was a clip that was connected by a cable to the small box, like a portable T.V. set, that indicated his blood-oxygen levels. Attached to his chest were two round patches wired to the heart monitor that silently flashed the green arcs and peaks of Raymond's heartbeat.

An X ray had just been taken of his skull where a small bump showed where he'd hit the volleyball pole. Now, the doctor was waiting impatiently for that X ray to be developed.

* * *

Only thirty-five minutes had gone by since the ambulance had sped away from Haliburton Junior High. Most of the students were still in the gymnasium, but the volleyball game had not continued. No one felt like doing anything anymore. All they could think about was Raymond and how lifeless he had looked.

Ms. Harrison had resumed her search for Miss Hiss, quietly now, and alone. It was just as well that way. A search party could have frightened the boa even more than it probably already was.

She unlocked the door of the empty home economics room just as the P.A. system clicked on: "Would all students and teachers please assemble in the gymnasium before afternoon classes begin." Ms. Harrison closed the door and hurried away in the direction of the gym.

Miss Hiss had lifted her head at the sound of the door opening and closing. Mingled with the musty heat of the hot-water pipe was the faint, yet distinct, smell of . . . of what? Something . . . something small . . . perhaps furry. Definitely delectable. Maybe a mouse!

She turned in the direction of one particular kitchen cupboard. Then she slithered down and down and down. Silently she slipped and slid along the tile floor until her senses told her to stop. Lunch was inches away.

* * *

Wilson came out of the washroom with Terry and Jay behind him. They arrived back in the gym just as the vice-principal was asking everyone to sit on the floor. She had a smile pasted on her face as if to let people know that what she had to say was serious but not impossibly serious. Not tragic serious.

"We have just had word from the hospital that Raymond is resting comfortably. As far as doctors can tell, this is not a life-threatening situation." Ms. Cameron paused. "We have that to be grateful for. I know you all have concern for your fellow student. The staff shares those same concerns with you. As soon as Raymond regains consciousness, the doctors will be better able to assess his condition and give us more concrete details. His parents —"

At the words "regains consciousness," a murmur started to grow in the gym.

"There is no need for any of you to be distressed. Raymond is in the care of very fine doctors and nurses. His parents are with him." She cleared her throat with a delicate cough. "Yet we must all cooperate this afternoon to furnish some answers to questions which I'm sure Raymond's parents have. We all have. What happened? Who was involved? No one should feel to blame for what was clearly an accident. Please come forward to tell me, or tell your teachers, anything you saw, anything you know. Your cooperation may be the best way to speed Raymond on the road to recovery. Thank you for your attention. At the bell, would you proceed to your first class of the afternoon."

On purpose, Ms. Cameron had not mentioned the boa constrictor. There was enough tension in her school without that. And how long could that snake remain lost anyway?

Wilson shot a look at Terry and then at Jay. His look repeated the threat he had made in the washroom. Then he turned and strolled to math class.

Ms. Harrison went back down to the home economics lab to resume her search, arriving just as the home ec teacher was opening the door to let in her class.

"I'll take a quick peek in here before you begin," said Ms. Harrison. She avoided the mention of the words "snake" or "boa constrictor" or even the name of her dear pet.

Everyone stepped back, and Ms. Harrison walked into the room alone. "Oh!" she exclaimed. It was a sound of joy, of relief, of surprise. There, only a few feet away and seeming to slide happily toward her owner, was Miss Hiss!

But out in the hallway the "Oh!" had had a different ring to it: panic, fear, shock!

Screams reverberated and students scattered. The commotion startled the snake and confused its owner. In such a situation, things happen. Things that are out of the ordinary. Things that can change the direction of life forever.

Ms. Harrison was about to bend down to caress her pet. Miss Hiss was about to slip into the cupboard and dine. What in fact happened in that instant of chaos was that Miss Hiss nipped a stinging sliver into her owner's arm.

Another shout bounced into the hallway. In an electric moment, the whole school knew that the boa constrictor had bitten Ms. Harrison. Who would be next!!?

Luckily, Ms. Harrison understood a boa bite and knew that the harm was more to her heart than her right arm. There was no poison. It had been an accident brought on by surprise, fear, and the unfamiliar. In her glass cage, Miss Hiss would never have made such a sad error.

Stooping over the coiled body, Ms. Harrison slid her two hands firmly under its middle and lifted her darling gently into the air.

Mr. Saunders arrived at the door of the home ecomonics lab, holding a yardstick as if it were a sword to fend off any foe. But Ms. Harrison was calm. Miss Hiss was calm. In fact, the science teacher was grandly wearing her reptile pet like a fancy feather boa (rather than the weighty thing it was!).

The crowd parted as Ms. Harrison quietly walked out of the lab and down the hallway to restore her elegant Miss Hiss to the safety of the glass cage. Students squeezed themselves against the wall in terror. Teachers recoiled at the image before them. Mr. Saunders marched behind Ms. Harrison as if she and her pet were triumphant and he were an honor guard.

But the snake had bitten human flesh. The word spread. It was whispered in the hallways and told on the telephone. Soon it would be written on school board letterhead to Ms. Harrison informing her that, for the safety of students and staff, the practice of housing any wild animals (whether a scientific project or a personal pet) within the property limits of any school was hereafter prohibited absolutely.

Miss Hiss had to vacate the premises.

* * *

How could anyone still think about a very tiny hamster after so much had happened? Inside the wall between the back of the cupboard and the hallway, Hobo snuggled, alert to unusual noises and disturbance. Instinct told her to stay put.

Smart rodent.

There was someone thinking of Hobo, though. Julie closed her locker door slowly, as if it were a heavy burden. But it was not the door that weighed her down. It was Raymond first. And Hobo second.

She headed for the bus with reluctant steps. At least, if Hobo were still alive, there was no longer the threat of the snake to worry about all night.

C. J. moved over to make room for Julie to sit beside him on the bus. They were somehow closer friends today. When they were together, things just didn't seem as hopeless.

"Maybe we can get Dad to drive us over to see Ray when it's visiting hours tonight. I bet he'll be okay by then. Probably sitting up and eating a ton of ice-cream or something." C. J.'s blue eyes held a glimmer of fun for a brief moment. "I'll call you after supper, okay?"

"Sure. Yea. That's a good idea. We're probably worried for nothing. Ray's probably awake and ordering double-chocolate fudge right now."

* * *

Instead of going home right after school, Wilson went for a walk past his subdivision, past the mall, and kept on walking even when he was almost over by the high school. Jason wouldn't still be there anyway, Wilson thought. He would've laid rubber about thirty seconds after the dismissal bell had gone.

Wilson was beginning to get a creepy feeling about him and his own stepbrother, Jason. It was as if somehow they were almost twins. This was impossible, of course, because Wilson was two years younger than Jason and they didn't even have the same mother.

But after what had just happened that day at school, that twin idea was starting to make a lot of sense. First, you had to think about a couple summers ago.

Wilson's mother was getting to be more and more happy with her job and more and more unhappy with her marriage. She was starting to travel to lots of places (China, Japan, Chicago) because of her law practice. It didn't take much looking to notice that she liked packing her suitcase more than she liked unpacking it.

So, one day she sat everyone down in the living room and presented her case. Or that was what it had seemed like to Wilson.

She was moving out. The three of them could have the house and she'd still help to pay for it. She would visit lots of times, of course. But her job took her away so much it didn't make sense for Wilson to come with her, and it would be better if the three of them lived there in the house, as usual. She had made up her mind about all this. She was moving out.

What she forgot to say was that "out" meant out of the country.

So that was one summer.

Then, last summer, Jason turned eighteen and his personality really changed. He took over like he was the boss of the whole house and his father didn't do a thing about it. For weeks, Wilson had cowered. If Jason shoved him around, he just tried to get out of his way. If Jason came into his room to take clean socks or CDs, he didn't protest. When Jason said, "Hey, Slimeball, give me a couple of bucks," Wilson did.

When Jason's fist smashed into Wilson's left eye and Jason told him to say he bumped into a door, Wilson did.

Now, today, Raymond was in the hospital because Wilson had turned into Jason's twin. What chance did he have of getting off this one-way street and turning his life in a new direction?

* * *

In the intensive care unit, Raymond was the only patient. Although the monitors were still in place, the oxygen mask had been taken off and he breathed on his own now, a barely audible sound in and out of his dry, open mouth.

On either side of the bed were his parents, both watching his face, looking for a change, any change that would help them to know what dreams he might be dreaming or what thoughts he might be thinking behind those closed eyes. A nurse checked his pulse and took note of indicators on the monitors.

It was already eleven hours since Raymond had fallen against the volleyball pole.

"You want coffee?" Mr. Stewart asked his wife.

"No. But you go ahead, dear. I'll stay here. In case."

"You'll need some sleep, you know."

"Mm."

"Eventually."

A strand of hair fell across her cheek and he leaned over to gently smooth it into place behind her ear. She smiled, but did not look up.

"I guess we should leave Amy at Mom's. She's likely asleep. Maybe she should stay there for a while," he said.

"Mm. That'd be fine."

"I'll check to see how things are and then I'll get us a couple coffees."

"Mm. Thanks. Give kisses to Amy. Tell her Raymond sends kisses too."

Mrs. Stewart was then alone beside Raymond's bed. The nurse worked quietly at her desk on the opposite side of the room, looking up every other minute to reassure herself that Raymond's monitors were functioning smoothly.

What can a mom think as she sits so quietly beside her child, when the only life she can detect is in the fragile warmth of his hands and the shallow breathing in and out? A flicker of light on a machine is no comfort.

A small song started in her mind and she began to hum it, stroking Raymond's limp arm. Then the words came to her: "Birds and bees and flowers, dah dee dah dee dee." It was a lullaby her own mother had sung to her when she was a child herself, a soft tune that made every nighttime safe and all her dreams peaceful.

"Birds and bees and flowers
soon will be asleep. . .
Hmm mm mm mm mm."

The lullaby was more reassuring to her than it could ever be to her son, so tragically motionless.

She put her head down on the side of his bed, still keeping her hand on Raymond's arm. Maybe she could rest for just a moment.

The clean smell of the hospital sheets was a small comfort. It reminded her of how routine everything was in a hospital. Even emergencies were routine. The doctors always knew what to do. Everything would be fine.

Quickly she lifted her head. Raymond had made a small sound, like a moan. Then, suddenly his breathing stopped. Finally he exhaled slowly, steadily.

When she leaned to brush his hair from his forehead, she heard something else. A mumbled word. A name.

"Amy."

Chapter 7

New Homes and Old

There was blackness, a seamless dark. Inside was silence. Stillness. Nothing. Time could not be measured in such a space.

Then, a light. Not a beam such as a flashlight would make, but a soft, comforting glow of orange that you might see just as you wake out of your dreams, and before you stretch and open your eyes to the morning sunlight.

Images. Colors. Were they memories? Or were they fantasies conjured up in that timeless, still place where thoughts fell from nowhere and words wouldn't form?

Green and blue. First one, and then the other. Down, and then up, in a steady rhythm. And a faraway sound of water gurgling past in a stream. Now blue. Now green. Up, and down. Such a feeling of freedom, of moving away from the earth and pushing high up into the sky.

Then, golden gossamer fins. Bubbles in tiny rows, up and up and up. Swish, and more color: shimmering greys with purple, pink and turquoise shining in the fluid light. Swish again, and silence.

And now, a face, small, round and rosy. Blue eyes squinting. A little mouth drooling goo. The sound of laughter, a high-pitched squeal and a giggle. Amy.

"Amm . . . Amy."

"Raymond? Sweetheart? Did you say something?"

The nurse put her pen down and rushed over to the bed.

Raymond made another sound, a moan, and then a whisper. His tongue brushed against his dry lips, but his head did not move, his eyes did not open.

The door of the intensive care unit opened and Mr. Stewart came in, carrying the coffee.

"He spoke! I just heard him. He said Amy's name!"

But when they all stood at the bedside, there seemed to be no change in Raymond, just the same shallow breathing, the same stillness.

Mr. Stewart placed the coffees on a table.

"You're tired, Lois," he said, putting his arms around her. "So tired."

"But he did say it," she said. "I know I heard him. It was just a whisper, but he said Amy's name!"

The nurse recorded something on Raymond's chart, then tactfully went back to her desk.

"Here's your coffee. Let's just sit here quietly in case he says it again. Okay?"

"You don't believe me."

"I want to believe you. You know that."

"He said Amy's name."

"Then he'll say it again."

They both settled beside their son's bed and sipped coffee in the depressing silence.

Raymond lay there motionless, the coma trapping him. How could they possibly find a way into that darkness to rescue him?

* * *

Wilson was in the kitchen when the phone rang. He and his father had been drinking coffee, something they had never actually sat down to do together before. His dad was listening to the whole story of what had happened in the gymnasium at school the day before.

Jason had not come home for supper, as usual.

Just before the telephone rang, Wilson's

dad had said, "Guess I haven't paid much attention to what goes on in your life."

When his dad picked up the phone, Wilson knew right away that the person on the other end was his mother. He sat there and listened to his father tell her the whole depressing story. Then his father fell silent. Wilson's mother had a lot to say.

"Isn't that a bit drastic, Thelma?" said his dad at last. "I mean . . . but . . . maybe it was an accident . . . I know that, but . . . I realize that . . . He's my son too, you know . . . Yes, but . . . Okay, then, we'll see you tomorrow . . . Yes, I know . . ." He cupped his palm over the receiver. "Wilson, what size jacket do you wear? Like a suit jacket type of thing."

Before his father hung up the phone, Wilson knew for certain that he was about to get off that one-way street his life was on. It would definitely be going in a new directon. His mother was making sure of that.

* * *

Ms. Harrison was alone in the science lab. In fact, she was alone in the school, except for Miss Hiss, and except for a hidden Hobo. It was 7:45 in the morning.

She stroked the boa's beautiful back, sliding her fingers along the scales, admiring the familiar texture and the precise pattern. Tears burned in the back of her eyes: this was the day her pet would be taken from the school and delivered to the Zoological Gardens.

Miss Hiss sleepily prepared to snooze for a few days, digesting the bountiful breakfast which her owner had just supplied.

Footsteps could be heard coming down the hallway toward the science lab. Ms. Harrison had been expecting that sound. It meant that the zookeeper had arrived to take Miss Hiss away. She closed the door of her pet's glass cage and snapped the lock into place. Then she touched the corners of her eyes with a pink, monogrammed handkerchief.

"Vivian?"

Ms. Harrison turned in surprise. It was Mr. Saunders standing at her classroom door, holding a small bouquet of flowers.

"Thought you might want some cheering up," he said awkwardly. Now that he was standing there, holding the flowers, alone in the school with Ms. Harrison and her snake, he began to lose confidence in his idea. Maybe she'd rather be by herself at a time like this. Maybe flowers weren't appropriate when a person was saying goodbye to a boa constrictor.

Ms. Harrison burst into tears. There is nothing like friendly understanding to bring painful emotions to the surface. And there is nothing like a good cry to wash away some of that pain.

She leaned against Mr. Saunders, sobbing into his crumpled V-neck sweater and his Blue Jays tie. Awkwardly, he patted her back with one hand and clung to the bouquet of flowers with the other.

* * *

Julie and C. J. stepped off the bus. A taxi was just pulling up in front of the school and two people were getting out. The woman carried a small leather purse with matching shoes and gloves. Her tailored skirt and jacket were a distinct navy blue. The boy with her wore some kind of British school uniform.

Julie and C. J. were too engrossed in their conversation about Raymond to take much notice of these visitors to their school.

"His mother said she heard him talk, didn't she? That must mean something, doesn't it? I mean, if he can say something, he must be thinking and stuff like that?"

"But what if she just thought she heard him?" C. J. wanted just as much as Julie for Raymond to surface from the coma. It had been two whole days. Now, the doctors were saying it was a new kind of coma, one that wasn't so bad because Raymond could breathe on his own and his heart was normal. But, to C.J., a coma was a coma. "No one else heard him."

"How could we make him talk? Maybe there's something we can do?" said Julie.

"Like what?"

"Like anything. Maybe send something to the hospital. Something he likes."

"Such as?"

"Help me think, C.J. Don't just ask stupid questions! Think of what Raymond likes."

"That gigantic tropical fish book."

"No good. His eyes are closed."

"Umm, well, maybe umm . . . maybe the new Pigs Are Gluttons CD. I played that for him on the phone a couple times and he busted a gut laughing."

"Hey! That's it! When he hears the Pigs, it'll make things happen in his mind, memories like, and he'll wake up. C.J., you're a genius!" She gave him a hug with one arm, balancing her books with the other.

The hug was such a quick one that C.J. barely had time to realize it was Julie's smooth face against his ear, and her soft curls tickling his nose.

As they headed to their homeroom, they saw the well-dressed lady and that boy in the school uniform entering Ms. Cameron's office.

"Must be a new student," said C. J. "Gross uniform."

"Mm," said Julie with little interest.

* * *

Hobo was sitting secretly underneath the secretary's desk tasting a sweet morsel of muffin that Ms. Francis had accidently dropped a few moments before in her hurry to tidy up. It wouldn't do for a parent to arrive for an appointment with the principal and find her having breakfast rather than busy doing her secretarial duties.

When she tucked her purse against one of the legs of her desk, the tiny hamster shuffled backward, careful not to drop its bran-muffin breakfast.

* * *

Wilson sat beside his mother in Ms. Cameron's office. He wasn't slouching. Nor was he wearing his usual black t-shirt and leather jacket, or his ripped jeans, or his sneakers with the laces undone.

Wilson didn't look like Wilson anymore. He looked like a British school boy.

He had on grey flannel pants, a maroon sports jacket, a white shirt and a striped tie.

His hair was cut short, very short, in fact, and neatly combed with a part on one side.

On the small pocket of his new jacket was a gold-threaded crest: Montgomery. This, as every elite educator and every prosperous parent knows, is the name of the most prestigious private school in North America.

"I am here to thank you for your kindness and your patience with my son," Wilson's mother began. "From the details in his file, I know Wilson has been far from a model student. I have enrolled him at Montgomery, not so much because of the academics, but because he will be boarding there. Away from the influence of his stepbrother and the lack of influence of his father."

Wilson's mother sat elegantly tall. From the velvet smoothness of her leather gloves to the gleaming gold buttons on her chic navy-blue suit, one could easily see that this woman was professional, confident, and powerful.

She continued her explanation. "You see, Wilson's father and I have been separated for over five years. My profession demands that I be away often. It seemed, therefore, preferable that Wilson stay with his father and his stepbrother. That was, obviously, a mistake. Montgomery will be Wilson's home now until he graduates with his high school diploma."

Wilson listened to the sentence that his

mother, like a judge, was handing down to him: private boarding school for the next four years. He looked at the polished tips of his new black shoes, trying to imagine what his life would be like and struggling to remember who he was inside this new school uniform.

"Hold your head high, Wilson," his mother said gently. "If you look down at the ground, then you will set your goals there too."

Ms. Cameron began to fill out the required transfer forms. It seemed to her that there was one Wilson leaving Haliburton Junior High School, and quite a different one entering Montgomery Private School for Boys.

* * *

That evening, Mr. Stewart brought the Pigs Are Gluttons CD and a portable CD player to the hospital. As he carefully settled the headphones over his son's ears, he tried to feel hopeful.

That afternoon, Raymond's two friends had come to the house to explain their idea. In their faces was such enthusiasm, such hope. Such naive innocence.

He would try their idea anyway. It probably wouldn't help, but he couldn't say no.

When the CD clicked to a stop forty minutes later, he gently lifted the headphones from Raymond's ears.

"I know!" said Raymond's mother suddenly.

"Why didn't we think of this before? It's so obvious! Raymond said Amy's name. Amy. She's the one who'll be able to reach out to him and bring him back!"

"I don't think it's such a good idea to bring Amy here, Love."

"She doesn't need to be here. We could make a tape of her voice!"

Raymond's father took a deep breath. The worry in his eyes intensified. But just in the same way that he hadn't been able to discourage C. J. and Julie, he also couldn't say no to his wife.

"Let's give it a try. It might work. It just might work."

* * *

It was almost bedtime, and Amy was in the bathtub splashing waves against a yellow duck that floated just out of reach. "Bah bah bah." She held her breath while her mom wiped the facecloth across her forehead and cheeks. "Puh puh."

Beside the tub, the tape slowly circled, recording Amy's sounds.

Then, when she was dusted with powder and snuggled into her flannel pajamas, Amy sat in her dad's lap to read her favorite book about the smallest rabbit. As his voice lifted the words from the page, she pointed at pictures and tried to imitate what he was saying. "Huh? Dah beh beh beh. Aaaaaaaa."

The tape recorder captured everything.

* * *

The darkness was wavering. Fluid. A motion that wasn't exactly light but which appeared to have shape and distance.

Images.

Words in a row. Black and white. Lines and circles and curves of letters marching past. Raymond's eyes made an effort to focus, to find some meaning in the parade of vowels and consonants, left to right, left to right.

Then a sound. Not words, but shapes of words in a small voice. "Beh beh beh." A gentle, soft, familiar voice.

His mind strained to make sense out of those syllables. "Ah. Dah. Ah. Ah."

Images.

A round and rosy face. Thin golden hair. A sweet smell of soap. Blue eyes squinting. A giggle.

Raymond fought against the blackness to understand. He tried with all his will to get outside the void and to know what those images were.

Suddenly, he had a sensation of sliding swiftly through a narrow, dark tunnel toward a vague, compelling brightness. He pushed air up into his throat. There was something he knew, something he wanted to form into a thought. A word.

He tried to open his eyes, but somehow he could not. It was like those times when he knew he was dreaming and wanted to be awake, yet couldn't break free. He concentrated on moving. If he could just shake his head. Or move his legs. Or say something out loud.

"Amy."

This time, everyone heard the word. The nurse rushed to double-check the monitors and to shine a small pen-light into Raymond's eyes. Mrs. Stewart clasped his hand and held it against her warm face. Mr. Stewart leaned over to watch as his son's eyes blinked and squinted against the nurse's light.

Raymond would be going home!

* * *

Behind a bookshelf in Mr. Saunder's room, snuggled against a dustball, was a small, weary creature. It had taken Hobo just a few hours of scurrying in the darkness to find her way back to that familiar classroom. When she lifted her tiny whiskered face, she could smell fresh woodchips and a bowl of hamster crunchies waaaay up there on the table. How could she ever scale the cliffs and crags of that mountain to her own safe, clean, reliable home?

Chapter 8

Celebrate, Celebrate, Celebrate!

Mrs. Warren was singing softly as she swept the floor of Mr. Saunder's classroom, her mind filled with all the recent events at Haliburton Junior High. Wasn't it just so wonderful that the young boy from this class was out of the coma! Raymond Stewart was one lucky fella. And that Wilson Reed. Everyone was saying he had been responsible for the accident. Now he was being whisked away to a posh private school. And the boa constrictor — oh, didn't Ms. Harrison have such a sad smile today — had been taken away to live at the zoo. My, how things change so quickly.

But then she stopped sweeping and her heart sank ever so slightly. There was the empty hamster cage. For almost a week now, that darling little Hobo had been missing. How could the poor thing have possibly survived?

She opened the cage door, reached inside, and twirled the plastic wheel, remembering the adorable way the tiny creature had raced and raced in there. The children had refilled its water dish and had placed fresh seeds in its bowl. Oh, how they wanted their little pet back.

Grasping the broom handle again, Mrs. Warren resumed her task, making skillful sweeping motions in front of the table and then underneath it.

Suddenly, a blur of brown dust seemed to bolt out from under the table and settle under the teacher's desk. Mrs. Warren almost let go of the broom! What in the name of heaven?!

The blur bolted again. This time it was scurrying down an aisle, and Mrs. Warren got a good long look at its furry round body and that very tiny pencil-point of a tail.

Hobo!!!

* * *

The evening television news was just beginning on the local cable channel when Mr. Saunders' phone rang. Mrs. Warren sounded as excited as a baseball coach when the team breaks a losing streak. As hard as it was to believe, for the second time in one day, a miracle seemed to have happened. First was the news of Raymond's recovery, and now that vagrant rodent was finally found.

Mr. Saunders turned off the T.V. What news could be worth watching after all the good tidings he'd already had? Maybe the Muses would inspire a poem tonight?

He sat at his desk, picked up a pen, and leaned over a fresh piece of looseleaf.

* * *

C. J. was finishing up a couple of easy math questions when his father called him to watch the news on the local cable channel. That was odd. When did they ever watch the news together?

"What's goin' on, Dad?" he said as he came into the living room. He noticed that his mother had a very weird grin on her face, like she'd tied a camel to the back veranda and was just waiting until someone walked out there to discover it.

"Just watch," said his father and winked at his mother.

They were both losing it, C. J. thought. Here he was, only part-way through his brief time as a teenager, and his mom and dad were soon going to be certified as unfit parents.

"Welcome to Channel 13, your lucky local cable channel. I'm Stephanie Parrott.

"Tonight, in the news, a tragedy has been avoided at the home of the Williams family of Dartmouth. Their pet cockatiel, named Albird Einstein, chirped and squawked at 2:10 a.m. This feathered fire-alarm awakened the white mouse, the two budgies, the cat, the German shepherd, the two Australian sheepdogs, the three kids, and the parents.

"Apparently, an electrical circuit connected to a computer near Albird Einstein's cage had started to smolder. It seems that one of the three Williams kids had been sitting at the computer for a marathon eighteen hours playing a simulated war game that had proven too violent for the electrical circuits to handle.

"At the sound of a sharp squeal from the cockatiel, the mouse squeeked, the two budgies peeped, the cat meowed, the German shepherd whined, causing the Australian sheepdog pair to bark and bark and bark. In no time at all, the three kids and the parents were out of their beds and the smoldering wires were safely disconnected.

"All this has lead our community correspondents to conclude that violence, even computer-simulated violence, is very detrimental to the peaceful lives of modern families.

"Now, on an even happier note, we take you

to the desk of our literary critic, Larry Lyric, who has the results of our Channel 13 Poetry Competition. Larry?"

"Thank you, Stephanie. Yes, we have a winner! Behind me, you can see the barrel of poetic entries which we have had the pleasure of pondering over. And, to our surprise, the winning poet is a local teenager who is undoubtedly on his way to a career in writing. Our five-hundred-dollar first prize for his poem called "Outfielder's Dream" goes to thirteen-year-old Haliburton Junior High student CLARENCE JAMES!"

Before his parents could voice their hearty congratulations, the air around C. J. became suffocatingly thick, his brain began to send wobbly signals, his eyes started to flutter, and C. J. fainted there on the sofa in front of the Channel 13 news.

* * *

The telephone rang. Mr. Saunders picked it up with some annoyance. How could he get any writing done if he was to be constantly interrupted by phone calls?

On the other end of the line was C. J., but he wasn't sounding like himself at all. "Ah, sir, ah . . . well, my father . . . that is . . . well, first of all I didn't take your poem on purpose. It was in my math book . . ."

Mr. Saunders was sitting down by the time C. J. had finished his whole, almost-unbelievable story. "Outfielder's Dream"? Laundry? Channel 13? First Prize? Five hundred dollars?!

* * *

The last few leaves of fall were hanging like red and gold Christmas ornaments on the maple trees in front of Haliburton Junior High. It was a chilly morning, even though the sun was beaming down upon the crowd of teachers, students, and the Channel 13 Mobile Unit as they waited for a certain green car to pull into the staff parking lot.

Finally, there it was! Everyone cheered, especially all the students of 7S, when they saw the small green car with the Jays baseball pennant flapping from the aerial. The engine coughed once and then stopped.

Mr. Saunders stepped out into the crowd of fans like a pinch-hitter emerging from the dugout at the top of the ninth.

Larry Lyric was suddenly there in front of him, pushing a microphone into his face and yapping on and on about what a great practical joke his student had played and about how enchanted everyone was with "Outfielder's Dream." Larry had C. J. by the scruff of the neck and was asking him to shake hands with his poetic professor. The crowd applauded. The T.V. cameras rolled.

By the time the bell rang to begin the school day, the chaos had settled. Somewhat. But exactly how much calm could you expect on such a day? Raymond was getting out of the hospital. Hobo was happily home in her cage. And Mr. Saunders was going to be rich, rich, rich! (Or so everyone thought — they didn't yet know the truth about the royalty rates for published poets.)

A small tap, tap sounded on the classroom door about an hour later, just when Mr. Saunders thought he was gaining control over the thirty-two teens in front of him.

Julie, with Hobo cupped in her hand, answered the door. There, holding a cake the size of an extra-large pizza box, was Mrs. Warren. "Last night, I made this to help celebrate the homecoming of your classmate, Raymond, and also little Hobo. Now, it seems, we're celebrating even more — your teacher is a prize-winning poet!"

Cheers were screeched to the ceiling. Bodies bounced and leapt toward the lights. Books toppled to the floor and pens rolled away out of sight.

Mr. Saunders gave up. For today, the lesson in literature would be left in his plan book. It was time to PARTY !!!

When the gigantic cake was cut, Hobo had the first nibble, some bits of icing clinging like snow to her delicate whiskers.

* * *

After school, C. J. and Julie waited beside the small green car with the baseball pennant on the aerial. Julie was holding a huge piece of the celebration cake carefully wrapped in a paper napkin. C. J. was in charge of the banner that 7S had made. It had taken them the entire noonhour and the paint was barely dry. Mr. Saunders was driving them over to Raymond's house for a visit.

When they arrived, Raymond's mother opened the front door with a welcoming smile. Behind her, carrying Amy, was Mr. Stewart.

"Raymond's in the living room. He's expecting you," said Mrs. Stewart. "He wanted to go right back to school tomorrow, mind you. We had quite a time convincing him that he had to follow doctor's orders and rest quietly at home for a few days."

Julie went into the living room with her offering of Mrs. Warren's celebration cake.

"Hold it a minute, sir," said C. J. to Mr. Saunders. "You gotta help with the banner." Then, remembering this was his teacher and the person whose poetic words he had inadvertantly smuggled out of school, he added, "Please."

They unfurled the banner. Reds, yellows, blues, and greens, all sprinkled with silver glitter, shouted the message from 7S: WAY TA GO RAY!!

Scribbled and scrawled all around the words were autographs of everyone in the class, including Mr. Saunders and, of course, Hobo. Julie had dabbed the tiny paws into blue paint and pressed them gently against the banner, right below the word "TA."

There had been a bit of controversy about that word. Someone wanted it joined with the first word to spell "WAYTA" but someone else said that it looked too weird. C. J. erased it from the board and wrote "WAY TO GO RAY." A couple of people in the class said it sounded too perfect, like an English teacher talking. Mr. Saunders seemed to ignore this statement, except that he smiled. But he'd been smiling all day, ever since the television interview with Larry Lyric. Finally, with one small change, everyone agreed that the wording on the banner was perfect.

"Here," said C. J., "you hold that end. I'll take this one. You walk in behind me. Please. Do you think we should march in? Or maybe just walk? I should've asked Julie. Maybe we should be singing."

"How about 'For He's a Jolly Good Fellow'?" offered Mr. Saunders.

"I don't know all the words."

"Fake it. Let's get moving. If we stay out in this hallway any longer, they'll think we've lost our tickets to the game."

C. J. started walking as Mr. Saunders began to bellow, "For he's a jolly good fellow. For he's a jolly good fellow."

Then everyone was joining in, "For he's a jolly good felllloooow, which nobody can deny." Even Amy was adding to the parade by clapping her tiny hands. "Which nobody can deny. Which nobody can deny. For Ray's a jolly good fellow. For Ray's a jolly good fellow. For Ray's a jolly good felllloooow, whiiiich nobody can deny."

"Hooray," everyone shouted, and then laughed.

Julie passed the celebration cake to Raymond. Mr. Stewart handed Amy to her mother and went to the kitchen to get some tape. Soon the banner was secured across one wall, covering two paintings and the light switch.

"My my my," said Mrs. Stewart. "Now isn't that lovely. And all those silver flecks of glitter. Beautiful."

"Everyone autographed it," said Julie. "Look, there's Hobo's paw prints. And my name's right beside hers. And there's C. J.'s. That's Mr. Saunders' over there."

"Hey," said C. J. "That's the autograph of a famous poet!"

Everybody laughed again.

"So how're you feeling now, Raymond?" said Mr. Saunders. "Ready to get back into the game?"

"Mom says I have to wait."

"His doctor's orders," repeated Mrs. Stewart defensively. "But by Monday, we think he'll be back at school. I don't like him to miss too much time with exams coming up."

"Ugh, Mom, don't mention exams! I'll have another headache!"

"Speaking of headaches," said C. J., "anyone tell you about Wilson?"

Raymond thought of the taunting, the dance ticket, the money, the menacing mean- ness of Wilson. There was no way it had been an accident when he'd plowed into Raymond that day in the gym. But who could prove it? When he tried to picture Wilson in that private school, he imagined stern headmasters and studious young boys, cafeteria line-ups and bowls of gruel, rows of uncomfortable beds and lights out at ten. Life from now on would sure be different for Wilson!

The cell-phone on the coffee table rang, as if on cue, and Mrs. Stewart answered it. "Raymond? Yes, he's home. In fact he's sitting right here on the sofa. Who may I say is calling?"

Everyone watched. Everyone waited.

"It's Wilson Reed," she said simply and handed the phone to Raymond.

The strange coincidence stunned them all.

Although they could hear one side of the conversation, they wanted the details as soon as Raymond pressed the off button.

"He's on a plane. With his mother. She let him call from one of those phones on the back of the seat. He said he was sorry. That it was him for sure who bumped me but he didn't mean for the coma to happen. And then he said how he hoped I wouldn't get any headaches and stuff from where I hit my head. So that's when I told him the part about how my skull was made of rubber, and he laughed even though it was a lame joke. Weird, hey?"

"Weirder than weird," said C. J.

"Weirdest," said Julie.

Suddenly Raymond felt significantly better. And hugely hungry. He raised the celebration cake to his mouth and filled his face with chewy chocolate.

His parents were smiling at him and thinking about the miracle of their son's quick recovery.

Amy was drooling and thinking about whether everyone would soon sing another song so she could clap her hands.

Mr. Saunders was sighing contentedly and thinking about finally seeing his poem, "Outfielder's Dream," in print.

C. J. was trying not to think about that love letter he'd written to Julie from Raymond. Eventually, he'd have to explain to his best friend what he'd done and why. The scene he conjured in his mind wasn't a pretty one.

And Julie was thinking about how everything was turning out just like in the movies — happily ever after.

Epilogue

In novels, as in life, time passes. Just when you think spring will never come, the snow has melted and robins are whistling from branches. You have a birthday. And you have another birthday.

These people who walked the halls of Haliburton Junior High, or slumped in desks, or gave the tests, or swept the classrooms clean, all continued on with their own special lives. So did the tiny and the looong creatures.

Mrs. Warren became head custodian for the school district. This was a desk job — someone else swept the floors of Haliburton Junior High. But she liked those occasional times when she came back to the school for inspection and remembered the good old days (and nights) she had spent there, sliding the wide mop over the tiled floors.

Mr. Saunders didn't quit teaching to pursue a career as a poet. He actually started to like teaching a bit more, especially after he published his first book of poems — *Extra Innings* — and after he got married. He had more variety in his life, now. The marriage was quite a surprise, even to himself, and it created at least two weeks of gossip and giggles in the school.

Julie did not fall in love with anyone in junior high or in high school. When she became a veternarian, one of her first cases was an emergency call to a farm during a freak spring snowstorm. As she and the young farmer helped birth the twin calves, something told her this gentle person who loved animals as much as she did wouldn't be alone on his farm for long.

C.J. fell in love six times and predicts that he'll probably fall in love six more. He went to theater school and now spends most of his time doing television commercials, comical ones such as the ad where he is wearing a chimpanzee outfit and declares that BANANA-

BANANA is the best frosted drink to quench a jungle thirst. (By coincidence, that commercial also required the services of another Haliburton Junior High alumnus: Miss Hiss dangles languidly from a tree behind the thirsty chimp in the ad.)

Raymond became a member of the Royal Canadian Mounted Police. He moved to Ottawa where he was proud to parade on national holidays wearing his red uniform and riding a regal bay. His youngest daughter has a hobby which she shares only with her father. Every Saturday, Raymond helps her clean the tank, check the pump, and sprinkle food for her rare and elegant tropical salt-water fish.

Wilson graduated from Montgomery at the top of his class. His keen interest in medical science eventually saw him become a neuro-surgeon, specializing in brain concussions. At the clinic where he worked day and night, night and day, some people said he was so dedicated to his coma patients that he was a saint, while others said there must have been something in his past which made him sacrifice his life for his work.

Terry and Jay are somewhere, but we have not been able to locate them as of the publishing of this book. Rumor has it that they aren't friends anymore. Someone said that Jay joined the army. He was so out of shape at training camp that they put him on a diet and he had to quit smoking. Someone else said that Terry got a job on an assembly line at a cigarette manufacturing plant.

Miss Hiss, when she's not doing T.V. commercials, lives in sheer luxury at the local zoo. She has an enclosure so large that she hasn't yet discovered that it is actually a cage. There are real trees and a running brook. Small critters scamper, twitter, and crawl around her as sunlight beams in through gigantic skylights. It's always warm there. At least twice every week, her former owner comes to visit and to hold her lovingly like a slithering scarf around her neck.

Hobo happily lived out her short life at Ms. Harrison's house in the country (only an hour's drive from Haliburton Junior High). The contented hamster shared a heated barn with other small critters: two families of bunnies, several chickens, a noisy nanny goat, and, last but not least, a handsome young hamster named Ernest. Hobo had a small litter one warm spring day. From then on, she enjoyed companionship, love, and motherhood all rolled into one furry ball of family.

I know you're thinking that Ernest is an odd name to give a hamster. Ernest, you see, is the first name of that little-known poet Ernest I. Thayer whose famous poem "Casey at the Bat" can be recited by baseball fans young and old. Ernest, the hamster, was purchased by Mr. Saunders the day before he married Ms. Harrison and moved with her to the country where, just as Julie had predicted, they're living happily ever after.